A Collection of Fictional Stories
6 different stories

Renuka.KP

Ukiyoto Publishing

All global publishing rights are held by

Ukiyoto Publishing

Published in 2023

Content Copyright © Renuka.KP

ISBN 9789362698674

All rights reserved.
No part of this publication may be reproduced, transmitted, or stored in a retrieval system, in any form by any means, electronic, mechanical, photocopying, recording or otherwise, without the prior permission of the publisher.

The moral rights of the author have been asserted.

This is a work of fiction. Names, characters, businesses, places, events, locales, and incidents are either the products of the author's imagination or used in a fictitious manner. Any resemblance to actual persons, living or dead, or actual events is purely coincidental.

This book is sold subject to the condition that it shall not by way of trade or otherwise, be lent, resold, hired out or otherwise circulated, without the publisher's prior consent, in any form of binding or cover other than that in which it is published.

www.ukiyoto.com

in loving memories of my parents

Contents

The Sacrifices of a Mother   1
An Old Service Story   8
The Night Rain   12
The Mourning of a Lady   16
Home Coming   20
Her Crimson Faded   24

About the Author   *51*

The Sacrifices of a Mother

It was eight o'clock in the morning when Amy heard the sound of the gate opening, she ran and opened the door. Sati, the servant was coming.

"Mummy, Sati aunty came," she called out to her mother.

Sati entered the gate, walked along the side of the house, and went to the veranda behind. Then she opened the plastic cover in her hand, took something, and placed it there. Later she looked inside and called out.

'Sir, I am here!' Sati informed her presence.

I saw, 'Come in', Amy's mother replied. Mom is busy in the kitchen preparing breakfast.

Sati is about 65 years old. She is a healthy woman with a slightly white complexion and a happy expression. She goes to work every day, works hard, and tries to make ends meet. Amy's mother calls Sati occasionally to clean the yard and the surroundings etc.

She took out an old sari and the scythe out of her plastic cover. After wearing a sari she wore an old shirt over it and tied a cloth around her head covering her hair.

"My little one dropped me on the scooter at the bus stop. That's why I arrived earlier," she said.

Amy's mother had already brought a steaming glass of tea, pudding, and banana.

"Just have some tea and start with work, "she said.

Sati sat on the veranda to drink tea. She took the banana, wrapped it in her plastic cover, and kept it safe. Then she poured the tea and ate the pudding. Her mother went to the kitchen pretending not to see it. Sati went to the yard after tea and started working. She is very sincere in her work and there is no need to say anything about it.

Meanwhile, Amy went out into the yard after bath and having tea.

"Where was my baby?"

"I've been looking for you." Sati called out for Amy.

"Taking a bath, let's pick up the grass, I'm feeling good."

After saying this she started to pick up the grass.

"No, your mom will scold me if she sees. Move away. After all, this will spoil your dress and hands, you just took a bath and came."

"Will the soil make you dirty?" Amy exclaimed.

"Isn't this my job, Amy baby? This is what I do. I do need money to live." Sati replied.

"Then my father and mother have money?" Amy asked in curiosity.

"They have government jobs; the government will pay them."

In the meanwhile, Sati started mowing the lawn and gardening. Amy walked along with her.

"There may be snakes in the grass, move away." Sati compelled her to move from the ground.

"Are you not scared then?". Amy showed her doubt.

"I have my fear. But the one who has no money will starve to death out of fear and disgust. I had not studied hence any office job. Your parents went to study in college and got a job". Sati revealed her helplessness with desperation.

Why did you not learn?

"Don't we need cash to study in college? We are poor my baby." Sati replied.

Amid the talking, the overgrown grass is being cut by her without any halt.

"What's the big news here?" Amy's mother came out of the kitchen and interrupted.

" She is asking to work with me." Sati replied.

"'No Amy, wash your hands and feet and go inside. ' Mother compelled her to go inside.

Amy is wandering here and there picking some fruits and flowers in her lap from the ground. Sati started talking again.

"I was working at the house of Thressya madam (one of her employers) last Sunday. She told me one important thing that all the elderly will get the same pension from the government. Is it true sir? she asked in wonder and continued.

" It is justified to give pension to those who have studied in college, passed the exams, and worked for the government. But Theresia madam says that 'others are also working either for themselves or for others just like under govt. So, everybody must be given a pension when getting old irrespective of their place of work. All old people should be protected by our government." Saying this she looked at her with expectation.

"Won't I get anything sir? Sati exclaimed!

"No such decision now Sati." She replied.

Amy was listening to their talk while picking up flowers.

"Then we should ask them to give a pension to Aunty who helps us."

"Amy, you don't know anything. Shut up," Mom scolded her again.

Amy's mother began to think 'Of course, it is true that I cannot do any work as done by her. I will begin to puff and pant if I do any work like ploughing the land for planting veg and plants using a shovel like her. I am also aware that the existence of all like me is the result of the hard work of these people. Otherwise, we need some mantras like in legend which is said to be given by the holy sage Viswamithra Maharshi to Rama and Lakshmana to not feel hunger and thirst while they travel through the forest. Or we have to find out medicine from the market for that end'.

Sharp At 1 pm mother called Sati for lunch. 'Sati come have lunch.'

She had made 'kalan' curry specially for Sati. Amy's mother pays special attention to feeding her. The yard was ploughed and cleaned by noon. Now it has a nice look to it. Amy did not come out from the yard. She was wandering here and there collecting a lot of flowers in her lap.

"Why all these flowers?" Sati asked her.

"Yes, I can make perfumes using these. A classmate of mine has said that we can make perfume after heating it in oil under the sun."

This reminded the 'balyakala smaranakal 'of 'Madhavikutti'(Kamaladas) in which it was explained that Kamala with her brother had made perfumes like this using punnakkaya.

"Give it to me also". Saying this Sati went to veranda for lunch.

Amy happily agreed. Amy put the collected flowers from her lap on the veranda and went to the kitchen.

Sati was sitting on the veranda talking to her Mom about the predicament of the house while eating.

."My daughter-in-law is cleaning at school. She will leave the place at 7.30 am and have lunch with curry from the previous day. Their daughter is studying nursing and staying at the hostel. A lot of money is needed. She has another son who is also studying. Her husband, my son is good for nothing. I struggle to make ends meet. My home is all damaged and may fall at any time. I want money for repairing this. This is why I am running like this. The panchayat has sanctioned a loan. Before repair starts we need to move to a shed and for all this I need money. This is why I'm working hard.

"Does your son help? "Asked her mother.

"What he gets is not enough to drink. Well, he is my son, I can't avoid him. Moreover, I have to look after his children. What shall I do?" she explained her pathetic condition.

Sati stays with her son, who has no attention to remember his old mother's misery. He is working during the daytime for his drinking. In the evening he would come and lie down somewhere drunk without eating anything, Sati would go along and call in vain and she would only hear the bad words from his mouth.

It is true that the mother is the name of the creature who loves others without expecting any rewards. His wife has also no interest in him who has no responsibilities and considerations about her.

Amy's mother wondered at seeing how happily this old woman is working with responsibility for the sake of their children and also she felt a resemblance to her deceased parents. She sighed for a while with regrets.

Sati is still active in her work. Amy is with her.

"'Amy, it is better to go inside without running around there. Otherwise, the beauty of your hands will fade away '. Mother scolded her and went back inside.

"I will take care of her, sir," Sati agreed Amy's safety.

The two of them again began talking about something. Sati showed her to 'fight' by plucking the algae growing from the palm tree. Amy was sad when she ate the "pottika" fruit from the midst of grass. She remembered, 'Sreedharan's friend 'in the tale 'oru desathinte kadha', which was told by her mother. Later, Amy was worried about Narayani's death, lying over the tore mat in a small hut under dim light. She told Sati the story of Narayani with great agony. Sati didn't understand anything but she responded with her gestures and kept encouraging her.

By the time 3.30, mother prepared tea and called Sati. The cupcakes and biscuits which were given as snacks for tea were put in the cover in her plastic bag and kept safely without eating by her. The mother got angry when she saw this.

"Sati, it is for you, I will give something else to your children."

"When I reach back, my young boy will run to me to see if there is anything to eat, It is to give him".

On hearing this, his mother gave her some more.

"No, sir, this is enough." Sati was reluctant.

"I have been told to go to the house of Theresia madam this Sunday as well. She has increased my wages. 'I hope you will increase my wage by 100 rupees as well". she pleaded.

"Yes, I shall". mother replied.

Sati continues to speak about Thressya madam who is her employer.

"She also has difficulties. The rich people also have their sufferings, aren't sir?' she looked surprised and continued.

"Annamkutty, her sister-in-law, will get a dearness allowance every six months, which she spends on a textile shop or a jewellery shop. whereas Thressya madam has no DA. Even though she worked for a long yrs. she said no one is giving her any DA. She is complaining even though she has all fortune."

Amy's mother: "DA, It's worth it for the low-paid. Annamkutty and her husband were govt. teachers and they have enough money also. Thressiamma who is an emigrant. No one is responsible for her pension or DA."

By 4.30 pm, Sati had finished her work and was ready to wash her hands and leave. Amy's mother gave her additional Rs100/- She found Sati's purse was filled with money.

"You seem to have enough savings?" she expressed her curiosity.

"I have been told someone will come to build the shed next week for us to shift until the completion of the repair of the house. The house has to be repaired. I need to keep everyone safe, marry away our daughter." Sati told her about a pathetic situation.

"Sati, you are suffering so much at this age, I expect at least your grandchildren to remember this. No matter what you do for our children, they think that we have to do so. I just said all these things to keep in mind. Anyway, do not spend the whole money. I am telling all these to not start arguments with your family. I just reminded you. You decide everything". Amy's mother advised her.

Sati has no time to listen to her advice.

"I need to fix that house urgently sir, then only I can think about savings". she replied.

Then she didn't say anything. Amy came with some champakka to Sati. Her mother also gave her some coconuts. After taking everything Sati went out from there to fetch the next bus in a hurry. She has to fetch two buses and walk another one more kilometre to reach home. She comes here once in two months because the value of Sati's labour is honoured and is paying satisfactorily here. Thinking of Sati's hard work, Amy's mother wished for her longevity in her heart.

Mother "god on earth", who feeds her children without having herself, and struggles to protect her children! Our generation takes that mother to orphanages and old age homes.!

While she was thinking all this, she finds that it's the parents themselves who forget to pass on humanity to their children in an attempt to earn everything and are responsible for their misery.

When Sati went out Amy came back after closing the gate and told

"Aunty told me that she will call back after reaching home"

'Well, I was going to ask her to call me. Anyway honey, go and wash up,' said her mother, and went inside with her.

……..

An Old Service Story

Aravind is very happy today. He is about to retire from the service within two months. It is at that time he got the news of his next promotion. How fortunate he is! As he got promoted and transferred just before his retirement, he was relieved from this office with immediate effect to join as Senior Superintendent in head office.

As a preparation, he immediately began to settle all his outstanding files and sorted out his notes and old files on his office table. In the meantime, he noticed a long cover. He took it and tore it. It was a story that was given to him by one of his seniors, Suresh sir to add to the magazine of which he was the editorial committee member and also, he was in charge of it. But the furious flood and then the pestilence which came one after another in subsequent years ruined everything. The magazine was not published again after that.

Although he was busy at that time, he took it out and read it straight away, thinking that it had been given to him by someone he loved and respected most.

"Service story.

Suresh slowly climbed upstairs to the office on the first floor of that civil station. Though there was a lift it was not always functional well. Moreover, this lift had hanged many times and people were suffocated for hours inside it. Then the fire force had to come to take out the people from it. So somehow, he reached the office veranda despite his ill health. The seats reserved for visitors were all full.

Everyone's faces were anxious and nervous. Boring of waiting. There were few people to get distress relief etc and also to get even gun licenses. Then he reluctantly entered the office and went straight to the seat of the clerk who was handling his file. Though he was a staff member earlier in that office, he did not expect a priority, because he knew well that a retiree is an unwanted one in any office.

As usual, the clerk's chair was empty. While standing there disappointed, the clerk in the next seat pointed out an old stool there and asked him to wait until he come and also added that he is the leader of our organization and always busy.

"Organizational leader, there is a rush and he is always busy. Even if it is late, he will surely come."

What can he do? Anyway, He sat on the stool, noticing how the centre of the civil administration is revolving there. when he was waiting for the clerk an old friend Prakash who had worked with him before came there.

"Ah, sir, why are you here? It's been a while to see you, how are you?" He renewed his friendship.

"Okay, my application is pending here. There was a small mistake in my leave surrender and I need to correct it and send back to the AG's office. I have applied for that. No action has been taken so far. I want to know the present status of it and to know what happened to it.

"Oh, retired then?" Asked the friend.

"Yes, two years over. but my leave to surrender is still pending with this office."

"Didn't you enquire about it?"

"I came here many times and also enquired over the phone. As it needs some calculations, they will set aside even though I had submitted a draft correcting the error for their easy reference along with the application. I contacted superintendent and the office head one after another in vain.'Yadhaa prajaa thadhaa raja'(how the subordinate, thus the superior). No one in that office dares to ask the clerk about it because they have to keep their comfortable seat safe always. Thus, each time I will be assured that it would be done soon. Meantime, during my visit here, surprising me I happened to see the celebration of the anniversaries of the government's good governance." He said emotionally and continued.

"Within this time, the officers have changed many times." After saying this, he sighed.

Again, he showed another doubt.

"Isn't it the digital age? It seems that there is no such effective supervision like in the olden days when the files had been kept physically." Mr. Prakash kept silent.

"Surprisingly, in the meantime, the office head also got an award for his good service. As a mute witness to all these, my application was sitting on the clerk's table ironically laughing." He spoke.

While he was talking with Mr. Prakash, the clerk arrived. Then Prakash tried to return saying,

"It will be the same for me when I retire. let me go now and see you later". He went out.

He enquired to the clerk about his application. The clerk gave assurance to him again as before.

"It will be done soon. Go in peace, sir. I will do it"

After listening to the assurance and walking back, the friend came back and said again,

"People in this office have a sense of reality. Those who come and wait for everything will get lunch free. Sir, just eat it and go."

He nodded. However, he did not go for lunch. He thought retired people shouldn't approach anyone with old friendships.

While walking back, some leaders of the employees who are just like political beggars came to see him while they are walking around and enquired about the matter. He replied briefly because he knows that they have no time to understand the matter clearly. They looked at him with a disdainful attitude, laughed, and hurriedly walked away. But he did not lose confidence and walked to the bus stop, believing that action would be taken soon for his distress. Days, weeks, and months ...He waited in vain without any reply. Even now he is waiting endlessly for a reply..."

....

Aravind read the story fully. The service story is always actual happening. Therefore, he was curious to know the status of his application. He had the phone number of Mr. Suresh on his mobile phone. So, he called him right away and told him about his promotion, etc, and asked,

"Sir, what about your file which was pending in the district office."

"Is there any decision, Sir?'

Hearing this, his voice became rough and became irritated.

"It had been given two years before the flood. The reply had been even drafted by me for their ready reference. They needed only to verify it. Still, there was no action. Then when the flood and the epidemic happened, my application became nothing. What is the relevance of my application when people are trying to save their life? But now everything is over. The government changed. thereafter I could not go to the office for the same. I have to refer to everything from the beginning as there was a total change in that office. Let it go", he sighed. "I am still waiting to see the granting of an award to that office for good service and also to see the disposal of my application because the applicant is no more. Until that let the file sleep."

Aravind felt sad hearing about it. Later he talked about family affairs and hung up the phone. He thought for a while about the administration system and the futility of the recognition of good work etc. There might have been more life-giving cases. Who cares about it? When he remembered that he is also a part of this govt, he felt a little shy.

Suresh Sir had a personality untainted by corruption. Therefore, there were detractors as well as admirers of him. But he is one of the many people he loved heartfully. It is a real fact that there is no use in knowing how to work only, we have to learn to adapt to the opportunity also. Otherwise, we will have to accept any kind of loss. Thinking like this the expired service story was torn to shreds and trashed.

It is his last day in this office. Relieving order has been received. During this time, each staff is coming and giving farewell to him. This is a regular view in government offices. It will continue to happen.

The official time was over. He took all his papers and got up from his seat to go to the next office in the new post

The Night Rain

The sunset. The daylight has almost disappeared behind. Twilight was mesmerized. It was raining incessantly outside. Devi was anxiously removing the window curtain and looking out from time to time. After a while, she saw the light of a car from a distance.

The car reached the courtyard. Mr. Balan, her husband came out of the car without taking the umbrella which was kept inside it and climbed to the veranda, wetting. Devi stepped out and wiped his head and face with the edge of her sari.

He entered the sitting room and sat on the settee there. Then he smiled and patted her shoulder. She asked him, 'Baletta, what about your busy, is it over? Balan smiled.

"No, Devi. I left everyone at the guest house. Food has also been arranged," said Balan.

Devi took from him all the files and placed them on the table. she took the hot coffee kept in the flask and gave it to him.

"Not so necessary. I drank coffee with them".

After saying this Balan sat on the settee and drank half of the hot coffee. He gave the rest to Devi. Devi also sat with Balan on the settee.

"It's not a good rain? I thought to get some hot when it comes." Devi expressed her love for him. Balan continued.

"What tension was there. The DGM was also there. They checked all the files. The whole day was behind them. Fortunately, there were no problems".

'How can there be problems? What problems could have for an honest and punctual man' Devi thought.

"Missed an important register, it was too late to trace it out. That was the tension. In any case, today's all over. There will be tomorrow too. It's a two-day event."

While he was sitting on the settee taking off his socks, he was talking about office matters and Devi heard curiously.

"Devi, I have to take a quick meal today, let me have a bath. After that, I have two files to verify."

Devi quickly went to the kitchen. After a while, Balan came to the dining room after his bath and began to have dinner which had already been arranged by her.

"I have to go early tomorrow; I will go to bed only after checking those files. I will be calm only when they go."

Balan was the branch manager of the company. The DGM and two Staffs from the head office have come for their regular inspection which is conducted every year. After his dinner, he took the files on the table and began to examine them. Devi sat next to him and started narrating the details of the day.

Balan was humming and shaking his head from time to time on her words even amid his work. After completing that, both of them went to the bedroom.Devi knows very well the busyness and sense of responsibility of Balan. She is also a minister to him. In the same way, Balan also does not forget to ask her about her food and health even during her busy schedule. Both of them sat on the bed and continued their talk. He said,

"You should eat on time and don't hesitate to eat while I am not there."

She smiled and sat close to him in bed and began to rub his fingers on her lap. After a while she said,

"I'll come after I finish the work in the kitchen, there's a little more work left." saying this she went to the kitchen again.

The rain was still falling outside. By the time Devi finished the kitchen work and reached the bed, Balan had already fallen asleep. She turned off the light and went to bed. She hugged him with her right hand. Then she slowly put her head and face on his chest. The hair on his chest and the smell of his body excited her.

Even though Balan was almost asleep, her presence touched his inner soul. He woke up and hug her with his strong hands even in that half-sleep.

Thus, they enjoyed that night. The rain was still falling outside. Rain is love. It's deep love to merge with the soil. The rain that fell in love with the soil was sipping love without letting it finish. With a melodious heart with ardent love, she fell asleep lying next to him.

At midnight Devi suddenly opened her eyes. Then she couldn't sleep for a while. She slowly took his hand and put on the bed like a mother trying to take her baby out of her lap and lay it down without disturbing sleep, and sat there. The rain was still pouring, as the longing for soil could not be separated. Devi is now not only a wife but also a mother to him. Different attitudes of Indian women!

At that time, she started to remember many things about the rain. In her childhood, she had used to watch with curiosity by sitting in Veranda that When the rain flowed on the roof of the house and fell on the yard, small pits were formed and the water falling in them splashed like crystal. When water was tied up in the yard, a paper boat would be made in it and would see it floating.

In her school days the story in Malayalam 'Oru kudayum kunju pengalum', had made her very sad. In winter so many children suffer from the consequences of unemployment and poverty on one side and travelling problems, various seasonal epidemics, natural disasters, etc on the other. So, she hated the rain even though she had an umbrella and other facilities on those days, she thought about the difficulties of poor parents washing their uniforms. But in summer there is such one problem of high heat only.

Does the government change school vacations during the rainy season? If the school vacations were modified! No one knows why the court's vacation too.

Aren't there many unanswered questions left in this country? Devi thought about many things and lay back again. The sound of rain outside was still there. Devi couldn't sleep.

Rain is love and happiness for many people. But she was afraid of it by thinking about leaking houses, old sick people, etc. Later, when they walked along! the edge of the field under one umbrella with her cousin Balan who was proposing to marry her, again she began to fall in love with rain.

As the rain fell in love with the soil, the love for Balan went deep into her heart.

Devi, who was lying and thinking about the rain which was raining outside, got into deep sleep again. Then she woke up again only after hearing the alarm. By that time, it was dawn. She lay down near Balan hugging him again. If she woke up without telling him he would be disappointed. She never used to worry about him, who loves her as much as his life. Balan was also awake from sleep by that time.

She reluctantly got up, removing his embrace, pressing her lips to his forehead and eyes, and placing hot kisses. Then to the kitchen for breakfast etc. Like a real Goddess! The lunch should be prepared and has to be given to Balan when he goes to work. routine started...

The Mourning of a Lady

The cold in the month of Capricorn is high today. The laziness of sunday morning is not leaving. Leelawati, who is a college lecturer, laid down under the blanket again relaxing. Her daughter Geeta is busy preparing breakfast in the kitchen. It is snowing outside. You can hear the noise of the children of the next house coming to pick up the falling mangoes from the tree in the south yard.

Though she lay like that for some time but got up reluctantly. By that time, Geetha had come with bed coffee. They enjoyed the coolness of the morning by slowly blowing and drinking the steaming coffee. After all the morning routine, Lilavati came to the front settee and took the newspaper of the day, and started looking through it.

In the evening she has to attend a seminar on 'Women's

Empowerment for their Upliftment' which will be attended by many eminent people. she is now at her daughter's house. When she was drinking coffee and reading the newspaper, their eyes suddenly were brought to the obituary column. Surprisingly, in that column, she happened to see the photo of her cousin Naliniyedathi.

The teacher looked again and again in disbelief. Yes, it was she. As if there she felt a flash of fear inside. Nothing was heard about her from anybody. How was her end? thinking about it she sat there for some time as if she could not move.

Her Naliniyetathi also joined the countless souls who were born on this earth and somehow managed to survive and hide in the eternal darkness! Krishnanetan the husband of Nalini Etathi, who was also a relative lived near her ancestral house. Etathi was very beautiful and tender and her wide eyes always seemed tender. Krishnanetan was the eldest of Sridharan uncle's five children. Although he graduated from Sacred Heart College, he was a very superstitious person. He had no love or faith in any living being on this earth. He had no world outside except his own home.

Now and then, there was a quarrel in that house. Mostly it was for some silly matters. made by her Krishnetan. She happened to hear all these from her mother who had used to say this when she heard quarrels there. Etan, who was working in a private company, would work diligently. Although he was stingy, he was strict. If there was a quarrel in the house, no one could see Etan's mother outside for several days. That was a big shame to them. So, no one would dare to question that.

Immediately after the wedding of their elder sister, they started a marriage proposal for Krishnanetan. If anyone asked about Etan's quarrel nature, they would say, "He was born in the early morning on a Tuesday. That is his anger. Shouldn't we marry when the children are getting old?". Then no one would say anything.

The parents pretended not to see the immaturity of Etan's mind. Otherwise, what can they do? In any case, the wedding went very smoothly. After that, the situation began to worsen. Krishnanetan, who was naturally selfish and narrow-minded, began to impose his preferences and selfish interests on that woman.

Amid that situation, the parents got upset. Actually, in all that time she was trying to laugh in front of others after enduring all the torture and isolation of their husband. When Nalini comes home from time to time to talk to her mother, Subhadra, she used to listen to their conversation by sitting with them. She would open up only to her mother occasionally

Leelawati still remembers what Etathi said once about him. He had told her "I didn't want this wedding. I needed some money. That's why I decided to marry because my father told me". The teacher now realizes that he was a narcissistic personality. Nalini had often told her mother about her husband's behavioural problems and how she keeps all her worries inside to not upset anyone in her own family.

His parents were helpless and could not say anything to him who used to quarrel over trivial things, torture himself, and cry. Still, they would blame her as if they didn't know anything. Many times, even though she had gone back to her mother's home, he would go there and making riot and bring her back.

Thus, her life was humiliating and full of physical and mental torture also.

One day when Leelawati came from college, Nalini was talking with her mother Subhadra on the kitchen veranda. Subhadra was very loving and if she saw other people's worries, she would quickly sympathize with them.

On seeing her, Leelawati thought that Edathi might have come running for some relief. Listening to his mother's scolding, he left the book on the table and went to the veranda.

'Nalini, there is enough money in your home and nothing wrong with you. Go to your home with your children. They will not change as far as they have no guilt consciousness. There is no other way to get out of it. Why such a life? They are not good people".

" Auntie, I don't want him to come and make a fuss there,"

" He is doing all these because you hid everything from the beginning, and now he has no fear. There is no matter in saying anything. Mother replied. Anyway, I wonder about his parents who dared to make him married. Now they are all united by leaving you alone".

Subhadra continued and tried to calm her down. After a while, she went back.

What a helplessness it is. Krishnan is fair to see and educated. But his immaturity spoiled everything. Anyway, he is fortunate to marry a rich girl by hiding his behaviour disorder. Leelawati recollected those olden days also for some time.

During their struggling life, she gave birth to three children. They were brought up with care by his family.

By that time Lilavati had left the family home due to her marriage and job etc.

After a few years, when she returned home, she asked her mother about Krishnetan and his family.

'He is still the same as before. But he will take good care of his children. It is a relief for Nalini.' mother replied.

Leelawati has attended many seminars and knows the experience of many such people. She asked.

"Don't his siblings have the knowledge to understand this rude nature? Will they not care?'. Mom sat down and hummed.

"Why should they worry about Nalini? When Nalini came, they were saved. It's true, he is selfish. I had advised her several times to talk about him to someone and find a solution for it. But she did not obey it as it is shameful to her". Mother continued.

She was right when we think about our society.

While she was thinking all this, suddenly remembered the fact that time is moving. She looked at the picture in the newspaper again and sighed once more.

She also remembered that in one of the previous seminars, someone had presented the helplessness of a woman who had lived with a psychopath.

Many people think that they can change their character by marrying such an immature person like him. But it is wrong and just like throwing stones in someone else's life. So if something like that comes up, don't hesitate to speak out. She convinced herself.

Now what about their children?' After the death of her mother, she doesn't go to the family home and knows nothing. The demise of a person who has influenced a lot in her youth, and also in the memories of her family home. She felt sorrow very much. She also noted with sadness in her mind that laws are often irrelevant in front of a woman's sense of pride in our society.

By then her daughter called to have breakfast. She got up slowly from the settee and went inside.

Home Coming

The time is five o'clock in the morning. The alarm started chirping 'tur tur'. Manu reluctantly slowly opened his eyes. Suddenly he realized the absence of the person lying nearby. He felt a little disappointed but then he was relieved. A feeling as if he got a little freedom somewhere inside him. He covered himself in the blanket and lay for a while and then got up from the bed. Then you can hear the sound of beating tea in Chandretan's tea shop.

It is the voice that has been heard for long. A group of people has been daily visitors there every morning with smoke on their lips as their 'peace of mind' and a cup of black tea in their hands. It is in that community that many of their very complicated family problems are discussed and sometimes solved. There is no shortage of defamation also.

Manu's wife, Rakhi, always wakes up first hearing the alarm. Manu wakes up when she almost completes her kitchen work usually. By then there will be hot coffee on the table. Manu looked at the table as usual. No regular black coffee;

It is true that she says that 'Manuvettan knows my worth when I am not there'.

Manu went to the kitchen and made a black coffee and came to the front settee. It was just dawning. Chandretan's shop seems to be busy. The sound of beating tea is being heard continuously. He has seen that tea shop since he was born. Although it has been a long time, nothing much has changed in that country shop. But some things can be mentioned too.

Since the new bridge had come, there is no longer the boatman wearing a kaili and old hat by rowing it with his long paddle. The movie poster with the picture of Prem nazir, Jaya bharati, etc. on the veranda of the tea shop has become a mere memory. And some such others have also been hidden from here.

Android has taken over everything. What changes nowadays? We can read, watch, and listen to whatever we want with a finger touch on the phone in our hand!

Manu finished drinking black coffee and put the glass in the kitchen. 'Manuvetta Sambar has been made and kept in the fridge.' As if his wife's voice was ringing in his ears. That's right, there is also the dough for idlily that has been kept.

Manu then returned to his daily routine. After taking a bath, he thought, 'Today I can go to Chandretan's tea shop and eat pudding and peanuts '.

Although Chandretan is old, his radiance has not diminished even today. There were two daughters for him. They were married and settled in different places. Now Chandretan and his wife are running the shop. Lalitha, the elder daughter, who talks very little had always been helping her father in the tea shop. She stopped her studying after school and continued it. Their only hobby was watching movies by going theatre in day time once in a while. At that time, she fell in love with Murali, who worked in the next shop. No one could believe that they were in love until they got married. the beautiful younger daughter also got married in fell in love... Thus, the marriage of two daughters did not become a burden to Chandretan and his wife.

Manu went to the sit-out to see if the newspaper had arrived. The Milkman has brought milk and left it in the house. Usually, when she is not at home she says not to bring milk. What happened this time? Anyway, Manu took it and put it in the fridge. Otherwise, she would be irritated.

The putt and peanuts in Chandretan's shop are very tasty. Sometimes when he was alone like this, he wants to go there and eat it. In the past, the main attraction of the shop was kappa puzhukku and undampori, but now it has changed to uzhunnuvada and pazhampori. When he was young, and when he used to go to the temple taking his mother's hand, he used to peep into that shop with great longing... there would always be seen as a black hot pot steaming in the fire with a stained cup and a sieve above it. Now he is using cooking gas instead of firewood.

Manu went to the tea shop after the morning routine. There was a group of people talking seriously in front of the shop. Sathyan Chetan was the leader of the group and was knowledgeable in worldly matters. When they saw Manu, they became happy and asked with surprise,

"Why are you here? Normally you aren't coming here".

"My wife went to her home. today I am alone here."

After saying that for a while, Manu entered the shop. There were steel tables and chairs had been arranged inside the shop. He sat on a chair there. Chandretan brought putt, peas, and pappadam. Manu enjoyed it all with great joy. This tea shop is always a nostalgia for Manu.

Sathyan Chetan who was standing outside the shop was saying loudly,

"Smoking in public places has been stopped. How secretive are we to smoke here? Only in the morning. Similarly, let the government stop throwing garbage in public places. How much-rotting garbage are they carrying away? Aren't they human too? People who throw garbage should be picked up and put in jail. It's the time of Android. Everywhere you look, CCTV and mobile phones. How easy it is to work out ". Then the other person who was listening said,

"That's right. If you ask them to pay a fine, everyone will pay it. If they are caught in jail, they will pay attention later because of shame."

Manu didn't pay much attention to the conversation and drank the steaming tea. He gave Chandretan the money and came out of the shop. Sathyan

Chetan was continuing his talks about adulterating the food and getting sick after buying it etc. Sathyan Chetan is so morally angry because his wife is a railway sweeper. Manu thought, 'Sweeping the garbage is not a trivial task. Many of the people would have a package in their hands on their morning walk to throw away on the deserted road. Manu returned by thinking that is it not possible for our rulers to improve our country by installing clean water and public toilets in every panchayat, scientifically treating waste, and making food security mandatory.

Manu opened the gate and entered. 'Rakhi might have called me'. He thought. She is calling to know if I slept well at night, had breakfast, or did as she was told. After leaving here, she will be very careful about me. Anyway, if she is not at home, it is really a wide gap. When she is there, even tiffin is brought and kept in l my bag. Thinking about all this he felt a little sad.

Manu took the phone and checked. Three missed calls. Thinking that nothing could be done because of this fifth estate, he picked up the phone and called back. She misses him. Manu knows it well.

'What was that Manuvetta? How many times did I call?' she showed her dislike. It will be so that when there is scarcity, the price increases. Manu felt happy.

Anyway, let it go to the office today, and can finish all the pending work. He started getting ready to go to the office. Rakhi had made his pants, shirt, etc ready to wear. She had called him just to know if he had gone to the office. What a caring and loving for him. Then Manu's heart began to melt with his love for her. He immediately took the phone and called Rakhi to come back today itself. She suddenly agreed as if she was longing to hear it. Then he took his bike and went to the office peacefully.

Her Crimson Faded

Part-1

The big iron gate in front of that house was pushed open and the white Honda City car came to the yard with a little noise. Hearing the sound, her parents quickly ran to the porch with joy.

"Come, children, how many days have you seen both of you,"

They greeted their children by getting reached the yard. Seeing their children, the eyes of the parents shone with tears of joy. Since they had been informed that they would come, both of them had their eyes on the gate since morning.

Their daughter, Viji was the first to open the door and come down, seeing her father and mother, she quickly held them together and hugged them. In that wide yard, there was a beautiful shade of various flower trees planted there. When stood in the shade in the yard, what a pleasure! What a feeling! She sniffed and opened her nose and savoured the scent and air lingering there. What nostalgia!

By that time, Sumesh slowly opened the door after parking the car in the shed. He took some packages kept in the car and everyone went to the porch.

"Uncle and aunt are coming to see you. They will arrive now".

"Oh, well, let's see them." She shared her happiness.

As soon as he stepped on the porch, Viji felt very happy and peaceful. It has been only two months since the wedding.

"Come Sumeshetta" She took Sumesh's hand and sat him on the sofa. She also sat beside him

The parents also sat on the sofa along with their children.

"Mother had been looking at the gate since morning because she is in a hurry to see you. And was the trip good? "The father asked.

Their conversation was like coming back from a long journey.

"What a block it was on the road Dad or we would have reached earlier". replied Sumesh

"Father and mother are well, children?" asked the mother

"Oh, everyone is fine". Again, Sumesh answered.

Viji is generally cheerful. Actually, she is a laughing box itself. Her long curly hair, her rose-coloured chubby cheeks, and the red colour Sindhoor on her forehead will attract everyone to look at her once more. Her mother watched her hair and told.

" I wanted to give you the pea powder. But later I thought it would be done next time."

Anyway, they were relieved to see that both the children were happy.

" Bhanu quickly gives the children something to drink". Asked her father to her mother.

Mother hurriedly went to the kitchen and brought the mango juice kept in the fridge and gave it to both of them. Then she said to Sumesh.

" Here is our mango, I was waiting to serve its juice to you ".

It was very sweet. Both of them drank the juice eagerly. Sumesh's face suddenly became joyful.

"How is your illness?" Viji asked her father.

"That is going without any problem, my daughter. I just want to see that you are all fine.

'When my daughter was staying in the hostel, she used to call and talk to me every day. Every week, my daughter would come home. Now it's been two months since I openly talked to her.' Father thought in his mind.

Even though he was slightly anxious, he hadn't shown it on his face. They were anxious about their daughter and allowed her to get familiar with the new house and the environment without making any disturbance to her even by a phone call. Remembering that Viji should not have any trouble there because of them, they had said,

"Don't always call, just call if you need something".

"Let Sumesh change his dress, I am going to the kitchen to get food ready. "mother said,

Saying this mother went to the kitchen. By that time uncle and aunt arrived. Sumesh and Viji went to their room after their likeful talk with them. Mother and aunt went to the kitchen.

Viji, who is studying Ayurvedic medicine, had many proposals. But, when the suggestion of Sumesh came, who works as an inspector in the motor vehicle department, her father said.

"When she gets old, there will not be any deficiency for kotamchukadi (an oil for massage). Let's do this." All the family members agreed.

Until then, they wanted an Ayurveda doctor. Now when they heard that it was a govt job, they changed their mind. Is it to get kotamchukadi or is it the local 'chillera'(something like a bribe) that attracts everyone to the govt job? Or is it like the mischievous Viji says that she should take a leave after getting a govt job as she used to imitate some actors? Anyway, the marriage was conducted auspicious

By the time she changed her dress, her aunt and mother had already arranged tea and sweets on the table. Father and uncle were also there.

'Come all, let's have tea,' she invited everyone to drink tea.

There were all the sweets she likes. Viji started eating each one greedily. He took some and handed it to Sumesh. She asked her mother while drinking tea.

"Mom, my right eye is always blinking. what is it?

"It is a bad omen; it is said as a sign of any bad thing coming.

To be continued…

Part- 2

While drinking tea, Father started inquiring about their well-being again, searching.

"How's work going?"

"There is no time for anything Father, always busy. She complains and complains when I get home after duty. As she doesn't have a job, she doesn't understand what I say"

Although Viji got good marks in all classes and passed the entrance test, his rank little dropped. So, he got admission to Ayurveda only. They fixed this marriage after agreeing to complete her studies as the proposal came before the course was over. One hundred and one Pavan gold and a Honda City car were given as dowry. Now he is talking about joblessness. Anyway, everybody neglected that talk and drank tea happily. Then Sumesh started again.

"She always thinks about going home. Mother should tell her not to do so."

As some poet has sung, honeymoon is when we should be able to enjoy and pour the sweetness of the love and romance of our spouse by wanting and loving each other! But now here everything she does think of as a mistake. They thought in their mind.

"All girls are like that. Isn't it the first time in so many days that she has been away from home? That will be fine." Mother made it a simple thing.

The aunt then changed the subject by talking about the busyness of work. Our neighbour Sreedevi who is living near us on the north side gets up at dawn and begins to work in the kitchen. She finishes all the household work and goes to duty at eight o'clock in the morning. Then it is her husband who is dropping their children at their daycare on his way to his office. He comes back only at seven o'clock in the evening. What a difficult it will be. isn't it?

Then Uncle said,

"Let me ask one thing, in our state with three and a half crore people, why is the government giving jobs and all the benefits only to some insignificant people and making them suffer? The work should be halved and the salary should be halved, then there will get jobs for so many people. wouldn't the government also get the services of double the people? Now the work done by one person should be given to two people in two shifts. You can go to work at one time and can take care of your family at another time you can do other work like farming bringing up cows etc. Moreover, the needs of the people will be solved quickly. Doesn't everyone go to work only to support their family? Isn't it?"

"Well said, uncle.

Uncle is correct. But the government workers will not like it. It's true. Everyone likes to reduce their work, but will they like to reduce their money?" said Sumesh.

The conversation stopped there.

Sumesh was enjoying all the dishes. No matter whenever he got anything, he would sit down and eat it slowly with patience. Is it his respect for food or greed and miserliness?

When she got up after drinking tea and went to the kitchen, her mother said

"You go to Sumesh; otherwise, won't he get bored.? I have already done all the work in the kitchen". "That's right" The Aunt supported.

Viji called Sumesh and went to the yard. Various types of flowering plants had been planted on both sides from the gate to the porch. Her 'divine mother' bougainvillea next to the gate seemed to overwhelm her. By touching all the plants, she had planted and cared for, and talking to them kinnaram, they walked around shoulder to shoulder in the yard. Both of them were highly enjoying those moments.

It is a wide ground and in the middle of it is this old family house. There are walls on all four sides and full of trees and plants. The place where she spent the summer with all her friends. In her school days, she used to run and play all over the ground to catch the small butterflies, etc. there.

Doesn't all in this land want to visit once again that courtyard where all our sweet old memories graze? once again? We have to pay our respects to ONV sir and his colleagues who have put such a universal theme into pleasant lyrics and presented to Malayali.But Sumesh was not much interested in this matter. Anyway, He just heard everything by humming frequently.

They roamed around the yard and then sat for a while under the willow tree there. If anyone looks at them, they would compel to remember that Millennials ago, on the banks of the river Tamasa, would remember those kraunja twins who were sitting on a branch of a tree chatting and kissing each other's lips in romance. On seeing them at this moment it may come to anyone's mind the first verse of the Ramayana came to the mind unknowingly 'Manishada...

The arali flowers are withered and scattered on the ground. When she saw it, she felt a little pain somewhere in the corner of Viji's mind. She remembered with a warm mindful heart. Her uncle's son. He is now abroad. He is like her own son to his father and mother. They grew up together since childhood. They were used to sitting under this Arali tree and talking a lot. Can it be said as brotherly love only? Then he didn't come for a few days when these thoughts about the marriage started. His face was gloomy. When this marriage was confirmed, didn't both of them feel a sense of loss? Did they keep an innocent love that they didn't tell each other? He was always more interested in the buds than the blossoms in which there is fragrance and beauty hidden inside.

to be continued...

Part -3

In any case, she didn't have the energy to say that she wanted him. If it was for him, he didn't have any work after completing his studies. So, he encouraged this proposal that came to her. Perhaps he might have thought that she should be comfortable with whoever she lived with. Let his love for her be so forever, and also, he might have thought that he doesn't want to own anything he loves. Like the flowers scattered below under the tree.

After some time, aunt and uncle came to them and began to talk. They shared all the details of their children.

At this time, cooking was going on in the kitchen speedily. There are chicken, mutton, Viji's favorite mango pullisseri, beetroot pachidi, etc.

After a while, they invited everyone to eat.

"Come Sumeshetta, let's have our lunch.".

She took Sumesh and went into the dining room. The wide dining table was full of dishes. It has been two or three days since the house was busy preparing a feast for the children. The last week was cleaning the house and surroundings. The biggest wish of any parent is a good family life for their children. That fulfilment of their wishes! The family is now contented.

" Sit down. Let's all have the food together," said the daughter.

While everyone was eating together, a glass of water spilled on the table touching Viji's hand. She immediately got up and took a cloth to wipe it.

"Don't you see this, Mom, how careless she is?"

"Didn't I touch on it without knowing?didn't I wipe it? Is it such a big matter, Sumesheta?"

"No matter what I say, she will argue".

When Sumesh said this, no one reacted to this. Though he was hurting her, he continued happily as if nothing had happened.

"We have to go to duty tomorrow, so we have to return today itself"

"Ok, then go after dinner in the evening" They answered happily.

No hindrance should come to his work. Parents thought.

As for Viji, she doesn't want to go. She doesn't have to go to college tomorrow. It's the time of the exam. She just needs to study. But how can she tell Sumesh? She didn't dare to tell to him. She can't bear being blamed for even silly matters. Especially in front of her parents. So, she decided not to say anything.

Meanwhile, the mother asked her daughter about the details of the new house.

"He seems always angry, and cares only whatever his mother says, but when the anger is gone, then he will be loving."

Hearing that, the mother was relieved. She said,

"All men are like this, honey, it doesn't matter. he is loving.it is enough

Even though she said to his mother like that, Viji began to recollect her experiences. He doesn't understand even a joke she tells as it is. Didn't he study for 'Poly'? How many people must he have interacted with? So why doesn't he understand me?Doesn't he understand anything wisely? I have a habit of finding any mischief in whatever I see or hear. I use to say things like that with my friends and making have fun. But he? Is The life of the girls like this? Is this why they give everything they have earned to get married? Or is this just her experience only? Can she ask anyone about it? So many doubts began to be entered her mind at that time.

She began to think again

On the first night, she entered the bedroom with such a passionate heart. Sumesh was not behind any expressions of love. They enjoyed it all night long. But one of Sumesh's words shook her heart.

"There had been many proposals to me. Most of them were officials. But it was you that my father liked. I married you under my father's compulsion."

When she heard that, she felt as if the soil beneath her feet was washed away. Then she felt like asking, 'Why did you bother me if someone had been there you liked?'

There were two children in Sumesh's house. The elder is Sumesh and the younger is Sushmita. Sushmita is married and now lives in her husband's house. She sometimes calls Viji.

Sumesh was born and brought up in another house. His grandfather's brother who had lived right next to that house was quarrelsome and was always had a boundary dispute with them since long ago. There used to be a big fight whenever they built a fence. They used to make fun of calling each other double names. Even though another neighbour was also their relative they were mostly loyal to the other family. Sumesh was born and brought up in such a situation. There was always a tug of war that persisted. Sumesh had a distance in his mind from all the others. But their daughter was the opposite of it. She was everyone's darling. She gets along with anyone easily. She was growing up singing and dancing etc. Once there had a big fight that happened to say that he sneaked a look at the neighbour girl when he reached high school. It was after that incident, they moved to where they live now. It is a nice house with a wall and a gate around it. After coming and staying here, he began to develop a tendency to quarrel and get angry suddenly.

To be continued...

Part -4

He has all the characteristics of a first-born son. He accompanies his mother to the temple. He helps in the kitchen. His mother shares all the details of the neighbourhood mostly with her son. While he is along with his mother all time, the daughter spends her time with everyone and captures everyone's love and affection. But He does not prefer it so much when someone praises her in front of him.

Once the mother complained to their father about his nature, he blamed her.

"Don't blame him, it's all because of your upbringing". She kept silent then.

Aren't they who brought up him without considering the mental development of their child? The daughter who grew up by her preferences without interfering in any unnecessary matters became the favourite of others.

Anyway, he studied and passed with high marks and passed polytechnic. Then he went for PSC coaching. He passed the PSC test with a good rank. Also, he got a job soon. He is lucky in all senses. Now with a good relationship got a wife also.

After noon uncle and aunt left, then her mother told them,

"Isn't he busy with work and can't come all the time, both of you should go to any one of our temples."

In the evening, both of them went to the nearby Bhagwati temple. She prayed inwardly to Bhagwati by standing in front of Sreekovil holding her hands on her chest

"My Goddess, please protect us always".

When she opened her half-closed eyes and looked at the idol of the goddess, she saw an extraordinary aura around it! The lighting lamps in front of the goddess suddenly seemed to increase in brightness. As if the goddess had something to say to her! Or just a feeling? She was amazed.

"Bhagavati please keep us safe". She prayed again inwardly.

Both of them received prasadam and gave the Dakshina to the poojari.

"Do you always come here?" Sumesh asked.

"When I get home, I will come and worship at least once".

"I felt a warm feeling in my body there. A great experience!"

"If we call, this goddess will answer our call at once. Devotees had many such experiences here. we can come here whenever we come, Sumeshetta." She got excited.

They sent their children to their homes after giving them dinner. Mother gave her coconut oil which was made by her especially and lentil powder separately. Also, some advice. 'You should bathe with oil every day, take care of your hair, take care of your body, do what he wants, obey your father and mother, that is your home now, even if you dislike don't tell anything...and so on.Mother's advice continued.

She has heard it many times, but still, she heard everything silently.

Viji is active on social media. She has done a lot of 'TikTok'. Many things have gone viral. She has not been able to do anything after the wedding. For Sumesh, all these are like obscenity or something. She had wanted to join Sumesh and do TikTok etc, but she shortly understood that it is not possible. He is busy with his work. He always comes late after work.

Months have passed. Viji is trying to adapt to Sumesh's characteristics as much as possible. It can be said that Sumesh is lucky to have her as his wife. If it was anyone else, the picture would have been different by now.

Then the final exam came near. Exam fees had to be paid. College fees and other expenses have also to meet along with it. She had already spent all the money she had until then. So when she asked Sumesh, he got angry. He doesn't like spending money on her.If she asked for anything to spend., he would make loud noise forgetting the premises shamelessly. It is a kind of blackmailing

"Your family hasn't given me any money, if you want, ask from home, don't look at me." He got angry.

Viji felt like a slap in the face. She brought a hundred and one pavan gold, a Honda City car, matching clothes, and all the other expensive items that were presented. It took a month to finish the sweets like achappam, kozhalappam, etc. brought from her home. Still, then Sumesh says this.

When she was staying in the hostel and need of money, her father would give her immediately in any way on just call.

"Do I ask the family again? What would I say and ask?" She thought, 'Are there still such humans?'. She wondered.

Finally, she told to Sumesh's mother.

"Isn't he right? The family didn't give him any pocket money, and everything in your house is yours anyway? There's nothing wrong with asking them. Anyway, I'll ask him," said Mother.

Later she heard some conversation between the mother and son. Anyway, Sumesh paid the fee. Viji was in such a situation that she didn't know what to do. Is her husband so rude? When she thought about all this, she felt highly disappointed. She spent all the money she had till now without looking for what or to whom. But now when she needed money?

Money is needed for many things to study. She felt bad to ask for money from him. Meanwhile, one day when her parents came to see her, she asked for money and they deposited the money in her account.

So, Sumesh was charmed when she started spending money on each and everything again. He would spend many things with her money. So, what a likeful he would be at that time. Is Sumesh exploiting her? She began to become suspicious and resentful towards him. She did not even want to speak to him and kept indifferent. Seeing his eagerness to spend her money, one day she asked.

"Why did you bother to marry me if you have nothing to spend for me?" Hearing this, he jumped by abusing her.

To be continued...

Part -5

"What did you say? Did You grow up to question me?" shouting like this he gave her a strong beat with his palm on her reddish cheek.

She cried loudly.He thrashed her again.

She was the only daughter of her parents who brought her up without giving any kind of hurt or pain to her until today. Now his hand prints are on her white cheeks. Physical abuse at the hands of the one who married her! alas?

The pain of the beating was on one side and the shame of knowing it others on the other side. His parents came running after hearing her cry and noise.

He is pacing restlessly here and there. when he saw his father, he started moaning.

"I don't want her, I didn't want her, you all compulsorily made me tie her up. I never thought that she might come to argue with me. I won't spare her; I won't let anyone tell anything like this to me as long as I live".

while he was shouting like this, he was also getting stronger and stronger and ran to her with his raised hands and stood as if to thrash her. His parents were trying to block him by standing in front of her.

" Leave her from here and take her home at once." Mother's advice.

"Get down quickly, I can take you home right now in the car."He yelled.

By that time his father raised his voice and spoke

"Nobody is going anywhere here. Let her stay here. You Go to your work."

Sumesh went out of the room. The father has some knowledge. He knows well that his son is accused.

Viji went to bed and cried. She closed the door but not locked afraid of kicking it open and causing a ruckus. Today is the day she has to go to college. She started shaking with anger and agony.

"It was enough to marry any other employee. There would not have been any of these problems. There will take a long time before she would have started earning as a doctor." The mother also showed irritation.

"Stop it, don't you have a daughter like this? you have to stop," The father reprimanded and started to advise her.

Sumesh became calm after some noise and quarrels just like a final of a delivery pain. She lay on the bed and tried to remember the lessons she had learned one by one. People with various mental disabilities, behavioural disabilities, and learning disabilities. When she thought about so many people, a fear flashed inside her. Oh God, is this all something like that? 'My Goddess, why does this test me? What did I do wrong? She called Devi and cried.

She remembered again. How politely they spoke when they called each other on the phone after the engagement. There was no lack of flirting. But didn't she ever feel that he didn't have the heart to respect others?

She lay there by turning on both sides frequently, thinking all about it, and fell asleep shortly.

After a while, his mother-in-law came and called her.

"Go take a bath and try to eat something. Don't argue with him. He just has too much anger. He is very loving and silly."

She didn't answer anything. She brought up her son as immature and now she confesses!

In the meantime, Sumesh took his bath and ate the breakfast his mother had given him, and went to duty.

She thought about everything and groaned and hummed and tossed and turned and slept till noon. When she got up, she began to think.

"Should I tell it at home? wouldn't they be embarrassed if I told? wouldn't they worry? It is better if no one knows about it."

She didn't talk to anyone and took some food from the kitchen and ate.

She was more traumatized with mental pain than physical pain. To this date, she has not brought any shame to herself or her family. Now she is suffering from defamation. what a verdict!

Then father-in-law came near her and spoke.

"Don't fight when he comes. He'll forget about it. Sometimes he is angry. That is all. He is very loving and obedient. Don't tell him any jokes. Just stay here looking at all of us. Don't try to argue. If you want anything other else, just do it."

The father's stupidity to avoid any problems. What would he think if his own daughter's life is like this? She felt contempt for him.

In the evening, Sumesh came after work as usual. Entered the room and changed his dress. His father was right. there was no such expression on his face about what had happened. She was sitting on the bed. He came to her and sat beside her. He held her hand. He stroked her face and spoke.

"I will give you how much money you need, don't worry". At that time, she forgets everything and leaned on his body saying in a low voice.

"My father and mother have not beaten me yet. It was the day to go to college. I could not go. I am in pain". Tears flowed down her cheek"

Sumesh's expression suddenly changed. He was agitated and told in a loud voice.

"If anyone does abuse me, it will be like this. Everything happened because of your deed

"Thonnyasa and Pokrittara. Everything is your nature. I will allow no one to teach me any new practice."

to be continued...

Part-6

Now Viji understood one thing. Sumesh came to her not because he repented or feel guilty about what had happened. No matter how much she thought about what she had done wrong just to get slapped, she could not understand. What is all this? She covered her face and cried.

He stood up there and shouted again.

"It should be better for you to stay at your home. I spare you only just because I am thinking about the honour of my family."

After hearing this, her last expectation was also over. There is nothing much to hope for. An outline of her life was almost clear to her. Later she became indifferent and almost silent.

That's when her mother's phone call came.

'Oh Mother,' she picked up the phone with a very happy expression and started talking.

"I'm fine, Mom, everyone is fine. I didn't go today. I had a little headache when I got up in the morning, so it didn't go away. I took a rest. Sumeshetan came after work and is drinking tea. what about Dear Dad.?"

The mother gave the phone to the father. She advised him to take care of his health and walk every day. After talking for two minutes, she put the phone down.

By that time tears started flowing from her eyes.

Hearing the phone call, the three people listened. Luckily, he didn't pull it up, she thought. Then she got up and got him some tea.

Sumesh's sister used to call from time to time. But after this incident, the calls stopped. Why should she stay here isolated in this house? She was worried.

Now Viji is not old Viji. She doesn't talk much to anyone. Especially to him. No jokes were told. Even then he would accuse,

"What has happened to your tongue recently"

"There is nothing special to say Sumeshetta, what can I say." She showed indifference.

She immersed herself in her studies and spent her time on social media when he was away.

The days were moving like this. One day, when she called her father, she got to know that he felt dizzy and was taken to the hospital. He didn't say anything in detail. Now he says that he is dizzy many times. She felt uneasy. He is getting old, Will there be something wrong with him? The more she thought, the more she started to worry. As it was a holiday, Sumesh was at home.

"Sumesheta, my mother said that my father is not feeling well. I have to go home."

"What happened to your father?"

"Mother said he was dizzy; it's been like this many times now. Let's go and have a look, Sumeshetta;"

"Nobody gets dizziness? It will go away with medicine".

"No Etta, isn't it free today, let's go." She insisted. He got angry.

"That phoning itself.no one should call from this house anymore." Then he got up and captured the phone. If he gets angry, his body strength will also increase.

But she didn't give up and insisted again saying 'I want to go. She did not feel any fear.

"If I tell you not to go now, then don't go, you know the warmth of my hand"

After hearing their conversation, the father and mother intervened

"If you don't have time, let her go alone'"

At first, he was reluctant but later he agreed to leave.

"Your best car is lying down, call a driver and go".

He was mocking again and again but she didn't care about it. Now it is heard that two or three times he is not feeling well. Something may be wrong with him. Her whole attention was on her father. She changed her dress and left by herself. Father and mother didn't say a word. It was like a whisper saying, 'Isn't her love for her father, let her go alone?' He said that the best car was just lying there. When she thought about it, she felt angry and sad, but her heart was full of his father.

When she reached home, met her father, and got to know the details, she felt at peace. she checked the prescription given by the doctor. she checked him as she knows.

"Why did you come alone, Sumesh, why didn't he come? Isn't today a holiday?"

"Something busy in the office. His father and mother told me to go alone. I can't tell when Sumeshetan will arrive. So, I went alone. I was told to call if there was any difficulty."

"But yes, he is a loving person," said the father.

"Let it be so", she said in her mind.

No matter what happens, just bring him along", mother advised.

Viji called an Uber taxi that very day and went back. Sumesh, his father or mother did not like this coming and going.

"How is he?"

"It's okay. he is resting." She didn'texplain further.

"So, wasn't that his trick to see his daughter?" His sarcasm again.

She didn't pretend to hear it.

to be continued...

Part -7

Days passed again. Suresh would go to work as usual. Sometimes both of them would go out. No matter how much love she goes anywhere, there will be a clash. She has already mentally adapted to this situation.

He always talks to his parents in a low voice without allowing her to hear all the details of the house. What is so secret in this house? She was a little surprised

There is generally no open talk in the house nowadays. There is no quarrel or noise but the loving atmosphere has been lost. Life is slowly becoming automatic. Now she does not tell him about any of her desires. At the same time, she fulfils all his desires without asking anything him. That is why Sumesh is very happy. she had heard that in the past 'Seelavati' used to take her leper husband to the brothel on her shoulder. She understood very well that Sumesh was keeping such a Shilavati in his mind. At the same time, she was also careful not to irritate him.

Meanwhile, the wedding of her friend, Remya who studies with her came. Sumesh was specially invited by her. They decided to go together. But she has to give her some valuable gift. She had given such a gift to her marriage.

"We don't want to play with giving gifts here. If you want, you can just go and attend, I have not been given anything by anybody either."

Another ayurvedic doctor who is also familiar to her is getting married to his best friend., she insisted that she could not avoid it.

"If you don't have it, I can buy it from my father," she said.

At first, he asked his mother to keep all the jewellery she had been given for the wedding. Later, Viji's aunt who is working in a bank intervened and help them to keep it in the locker. All the jewels that she had brought are in his locker, he drives her Honda City car by himself. whereas she is in a situation where she is not even able to pay for the bus money. Is there a life like this? She let out a deep breath.

One day he said on some occasion.

"How many marriage proposals have come? Despite having such a good job, my destiny is to get this old type car."

She didn't respond as she was familiar with such conversations. Moreover, she does not even know how much her husband's salary is. She does not have any such wishes. She gives in to his wishes as much as possible so as not to be humiliated in front of others.

Moreover, she has also realized that it is unlikely that he will have the common sense to know the feelings of his fellow man in this life.

But no matter how much we hold on, we will be weak in some moments. She didn't quite get the joke about the current old car. She said,

"If it's an old car, why not give it back and buy another good one?"

"What are you kidding? You're kidding me? It's a dirty car. There are so many nice cars. Remember that I'm a vehicle inspector. What kind of cars do I see every day? Could your father give me a nice car? It's my generosity to marry you up without a job. If you're polite and obedient, you can stay here otherwise not".

And then, in the excitement of those words, he gave her a hit with that strong hand. At that moment, unknowingly, a cry of "wicked" came from her heart. She did not feel any shame.

"Who is your wicked man, will you call me wicked?" Sumesh said again.

"Why are you mad?" she shouted. Father and mother came running after hearing the noise.

"What happened?"

"I can't live with her even for a second. Aren't all of you tied to my head? She should not be in this house for a second. Pick up the phone and call them to take her away."

Her parents are old too. If they hear this? She is totally upset to hear this. She got up from there.

She said, "Don't call them, I'll go."

But he took her phone and called her father.

"If you want your daughter, it's better to take her immediately. We don't want to keep this bastard here, it's enough." After saying this he cut the phone.

The phone began to ring continuously. It was from her home. He didn't take it and answer. He didn't allow her to touch it also. She started crying.

to be continued...

Part- 8

Physical abuse, humiliation, and the situation at home. She can't even think about it. What a helpless situation. How can she, who is an innocent, endure all this?

When she stays in the hostel, if she doesn't take the phone on call any day, her father will fly up there. If her face withers, they won't bear it. Such a nurturing baby is being tortured by him like this here. What a fate!

Isn't it because of this that a woman is called Abala? Can she not be Abala because she took a heavy driving license like a man or climb a coconut tree?

As for Viji, there were no such features of the new generation in her appearance or behaviour. Ayurveda, a part of the Chaturveda, was her subject of study. There was always a divinity on her face.

Sumesh's parents were astonished by seeing Viji's crying and noise. What to do, what to say, there is no way. Viji is lying there helplessly. What will they say to her father and mother? was it wrong to hide everything from them for so long?

After about an hour, the parents with her uncle, and their community leader arrived there.

The three of them were told with exaggeration about her quarrels, arguments, feelings, disobedience, etc with great disgust.

"If she is decent, I will be also. Otherwise, I will show her my real character. 'If it's polite', I'm again saying it." He is shouting.

"If this is the situation here, it's better to take her back home," said her parents with agony and disappointment.

They discussed all things for a long time. She still didn't talk about his physical hurt because of shame. She is continuously humiliated because of his wicked nature. Finally, she had to say it openly that he is arrogant and violent when he gets angry and always quarrelsome. She had also to reveal that she didn't tell her parents so as not to worry them.

It was very sympathetic to see the pity on the face of her parents at that time.

"A good government employee. Goes to work and earns a salary and takes care of the family. He does not drink, does not smoke, and has no bad habits." The parents were describing the character traits of their son.

After a long discussion, at the end of the mediation, Sumesh told them that he loves Viji very much and does not want to leave her. There is only one condition for him.' Don't argue.' Hadn't he any consistent nature.?.

Viji also explained that the reason for the current clash was because of that car.

"It's only when he gets angry that it's a problem or otherwise it's okay. I don't want to leave."

She also said the same to them. She said so because she was eager about her parents. From where did this girl get such strength?

After hearing everything, the leader felt that 'This is where all girls go wrong. They think of shame and endure everything. What is lacking in her house? But the fear of society and the thought of not worrying her parents. How much she endures for that!'

Isn't the lust for money and physical enjoyment by leaving the dharma, the cause of all the troubles seen in society nowadays.? Why doesn't our society think that way? Seniors should first know how much moral thinking is needed for life to be peaceful, and how much the desires can be in our life...

Mediation is now over. Still, her family has not learned anything. They decided to give me another car by changing it. As both of them were not interested in separation, the decision was easy for the arbitrators. unfortunately, no one mentioned the matter of his physical abuse. Anyway, some 'spelling mistake' was caught by all of them.

At last, both of them were advised not to get worse the trivial things by exaggerating and that both them should be careful in all things onwards.

Viji's mother wants to take her daughter with them. That mother feared a lot. She did not want her to stay there in this condition. How can anyone go back peacefully in this situation.?

"But then let both of them go there for two days".

Everyone again came to a decision. Sumesh also agreed with his father's compulsion. He has no such stable character. But his mother felt doubt.

Anyway, all the problems there are now over. The only thing that was left was that she was unable to go to the wedding. which she desired most.

The days were going on as before. Sumesh had no particular change. But she could not bear that her peaceless life was coming to be known by all. That was more agitating than her body pain.

His greed and selfishness. If it was not satisfied well, he gets angry. His love and his hatred do have not much life. he can't be believed and also can't be said anything with honesty as he lacks a stable nature. Who knows when he will shout all that? This is the last picture she has obtained of him.

She was slowly becoming like a doll. Now there is even no one to talk to openly.

Anyway, she had been allowed to call home every day in that day's mediation. She would always call her parents thinking that they should get some peace

One day when she reached home from college it was late. Sumesh had already reached by then. He was waiting there impatiently.

to be continued...

Part -9

"Where have you been till now? Didn't the exam end at 5 o'clock? turned off the phone and where did you go?" he asked.

She comes tired after waiting a long time at the bus stand. Her phone is switched off. It was enough to say that she was late to get the bus. But the harsh question irritated her.

"Are you starting to blame me immediately on my just arrival? Don't you know I was in college?

" Let me drink a glass of water. My throat is dry."

After saying this she went to the kitchen and took a glass of water. At that time, he came fast running and knocked the glass out of her hand.

"Didn't I ask you where you went? Do you want to make me fool without answering?"

"Oh God, I have come here to drink water. My Goddess! doesn't allow me even to drink a glass of water here."

She put her hand on her head and sat on the stool lying in the kitchen and started to cry.

"I am coming by line bus. I am not traveling by my car. It was late to get the bus. Aren't you that using my bad car by yourself?"

When he heard about the car, he was shocked again.

"Yes, it is your bad car, do you have any doubts? If you open your mouth again, it will be the end of you,". After uttering this he ran to her and gave a big kick.

She fell from the stool and lay down there. Still, his anger did not remove. He again kicked her on her thigh once more. She screamed.

"I will take the phone and call the police. All three of you will be caught up in the torture of the woman. But I am not doing this because I'm also ashamed of it." She screamed.

When he hears this also, he could not control himself. he dragged her holding hair and beat her on her head harshly with his strong hand. She fell and fainted. Without caring for her he began to shout again.

"Weren't you coming here to let us all in? What a great idea!

I won't let you go anywhere from here." When he was saying this, he was panting.

When no response was heard, he looked at her. He saw that she was lying quietly without any movement on the floor. When he saw that, he suddenly felt fear. He went to the kitchen stairs quietly. After a while, he didn't hear any sound or moan. He slowly come to her and placed his hands on her nose. No breathing. No sign of alive. He was shocked. Then he went out silently thinking what to do.

This is a glimpse of the practicality of laws against women's violence!

His parents don't intervene if they hear a small quarrel recently. But now they came to see because they couldn't hear any noise or movement. Alas! That old couple was stunned to see the scene there.

Later she was taken to the hospital. By then the 'story of her' was over. Then all the things that took place there are conceivable.

All the legal activities were taken by the police authorities. Sumesh was arrested and remanded for dowry death. His brother-in-law and sister tried their best for making it an accident by saying that she fell into the kitchen and crashed.

But that old parents could not hold with lies for a long time. The circumstance pieces of evidence were fully against him. Though Sumesh was low-tempered and immature in his behaviour he was very sincere with his own family. So, they could not suffer the situation. The whole family cried aloud in vain. No one is there to help them. The legal procedures were continued as usual. What about Viji's parents? Their condition was very pathetic. They were crying in great disappointment regretting that they are solely responsible for the disaster of their daughter by leaving her there even after being doubtful about her safety. Bhanumati, her mother was hospitalized for many days. She became delirious and took so many days to recover. Her cousin who was abroad came and help them without knowing her absence. His mourning by calling her had made everyone there weep.

"Viji, don't you have me, why you left all of us?" The people there tried hard to keep him away from her body.

Our media, including social media, gave news with speculations for several days with various poses of the sad people as if 'I am in front, I am in front '.

But some of their close relatives started some gossip with each other. There are no wounds that cannot be healed with time. After some time, they will surely return to normal. They won't this news be a pain for them? Is it our enlightenment to expose one's helplessness in front of the public? what a herd instinct of society!

Days have passed. Sumesh is being punished for dowry abuse. He was suspendedfrom his job.

Who is responsible for this tragedy? Is it Sumesh, who is a greedy and miserly person without having the power to accept others? Or is it Viji who thinks it a shame to leave her husband despite knowing that he is a man of low tempered and with not much morality? Or either her parents who married their daughter without enquiring anything about the boy and considering only his government job without even completing her studies? Or his parents who didn't teach him to be able to live morally with a broad mind by accepting and giving respect to all? All kinds of discussions were continued for several days in all media.

Months passed. Viji's parents are now on the path of devotional service. Most of the time they were on pilgrimages in different places. They are doing charitable work also. Spiritual life made them a new version now. But Sumesh's father could not be sustained the situation as he was that much dependable with his son. He left this world before some time. His mother was taken by her daughter, Sushmita. They are leaving their days somehow. The case is still under consideration by the court

Let the decree and judgment be come from the court. Let's wait and see the remaining part later.

Ended.

About the Author

Renuka KP

Smt Renuka.K.P is a native of N.Paravur in Ernakulam district of Kerala as the daughter of Late Sri.Parameswaran and Late Smt.Kousalia. After her graduation in Economics, she entered into the Kerala govt. service and retired as Tahsildar in 2017. Now she is actively engaged as an online writer in the open platform Pratilipi and has received a certificate of merit for her story. She is also involved in social media and has her own youtube channel. She clearly exhibits her outlook on social and cultural affairs of the society, especially against domestic violence of women. She currently resides in Aluva with her husband (retired Asst. manager). She has two children and both of them are married. Her elder son is working as an engineer in the UK and daughter, a dental surgeon now residing in Bengaluru.

www.ingramcontent.com/pod-product-compliance
Lightning Source LLC
LaVergne TN
LVHW041636070526
838199LV00052B/3396